SINGING LIKE A SONG BIRD

ILLUSTRATIONS BY SHONDA M PARKS

THIS IS THE STORY OF A
MOTHER'S DESIRE TO SING LIKE
A SONG BIRD. MOTHER LOVED TO
SING, BUT SHE DIDN'T THINK HER
VOICE WAS BEAUTIFUL AND
SHE DIDN'T KNOW IF
PEOPLE WOULD ENJOY HER
SINGING.

THAT SUMMER, MOTHER WAS COMMITTED TO
WRITING SONGS AND SINGING HER SONGS.
MOTHER EXCITED ABOUT HER PLAN,
SHARED HER INTENTIONS WITH
ALL HER FAMILY MEMBERS.

THE NEXT
MORNING, MOTHER
AWAKENED HUMMING,
(MM, MM, OH YEAH)

EVERYDAY MOTHER WOULD SING.

SHE SANG WHEN SHE CLEANED.

SHE SANG WHEN SHE EXERCISED.

SHE SANG WORKING IN HER GARDEN, A PLACE OF PEACE.

SHE EVEN SANG TO HER FOOD BEFORE EATING.

MOTHER WAS SINGING,
SINGING, SEEMINGLY
DRIVING HER FAMILY CRAZY;

SINGING EVERY STATEMENT,
AND NAMES OF EVERYONE. SHE
WAS NO LONGER HAVING
REGULAR CONVERSATION, SHE
WAS SINGING EVERYTHING.

HER FAMILY WAS
APPEARING IRRITATED:
THEY BEGAN AVOIDING
MOTHER,

LOOKING AROUND THE
CORNERS TO ASSURE
THEMSELVES NOT TO BUMP
INTO HER.

THE NEXT
MORNING
MOTHER
AWAKENED
TO
WHISPERING

VOICES IN
THE KITCHEN.

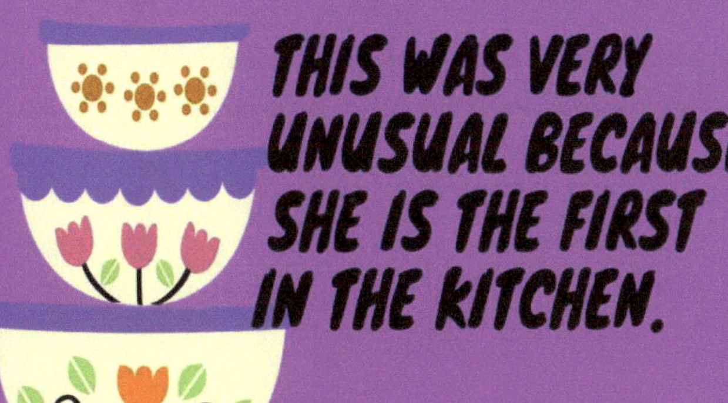

THIS WAS VERY UNUSUAL BECAUSE SHE IS THE FIRST IN THE KITCHEN.

QUICKLY AND QUIETLY SHE TIP TOED CLOSE ENOUGH TO HEAR.

MOTHER COULDN'T BELIEVE HER EARS,
HER FAMILY WAS EXPRESSING
IRRITATION AND WISHING THINGS
COULD GET BACK TO NORMAL.

SHE MOPED AROUND THAT MORNING UNTIL SHE FOUND HERSELF IN THE GARDEN, WHERE SHE FOUND A BIT OF PEACE.

MOTHER BEGAN SINGING, ATTEMPTING TO SING HER

BLUES AWAY AND TO HER OWN AMAZEMENT HER VOICE SOUNDED BEAUTIFULLY.

NOW, SHE BEGAN TO FEEL EXCITMENT AND JOY IN HER SINGING
FEELING GOOD ABOUT HERSELF, SHE CLOSED HER EYES AND TWIRLED AROUND WITH HAPPINESS

IT FELT AS
IF TIME HAD
STOPPED

WHEN MOTHER OPENED HER EYES, TO HER SURPRISE, THERE WERE BIRDS SITTING ON THE TREE BRANCHES, SITTING ON THE ELECTRICAL WIRES, AND SITTING ON THE FENCES.

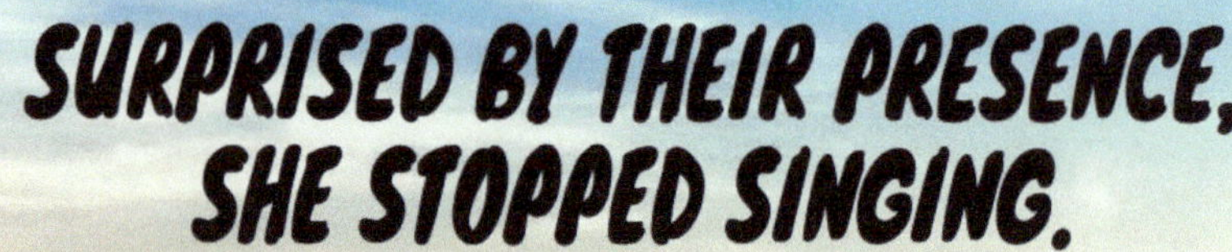

SURPRISED BY THEIR PRESENCE,
SHE STOPPED SINGING.

THE NEXT MOMENT
THE BIRDS
STARTED
SERANADING
MOTHER'S
SINGING SHOWING
THEIR
APPRECIATION FOR
HER
BEAUTIFUL VOICE.

HEARING THE BIRDS LOUDLY SERENADING, HER FAMILY MEMBERS RAN INTO THE GARDEN JUST IN TIME TO WITNESS THE EXTRAORDINARY MOMENT.

IT WAS AT THIS
MOMENT
MOTHER AND HER
FAMILY MEMBERS
KNEW
SHE COULD
SING LIKE A SONG BIRD

THE END

THIS BOOK BELONGS TO

____